Medusa's Scream

Melanie Jackson

Orca *currents*

ORCA BO

D1018599

Library and Archives Canada Cataloguing in Publication

Jackson, Melanie, 1956-, author
Medusa's Scream / Melanie Jackson.
(Orca currents)

Issued in print and electronic formats.
ISBN 978-1-4598-1441-7 (softcover).—ISBN 978-1-4598-1442-4 (pdf).—
ISBN 978-1-4598-1443-1 (epub)

I. Title. II. Series: Orca currents
PS8569.A265M43 2017   jc813'.6   c2017-900868-4
c2017-900869-2

First published in the United States, 2017
Library of Congress Control Number: 2017933021

Summary: In this high-interest novel for middle readers, Chase gets a job
at an abandoned gold mine that has been converted into an amusement ride.

MIX
Paper from
responsible sources
FSC
www.fsc.org
FSC® C103214

*Orca Book Publishers is dedicated to preserving the environment and has
printed this book on Forest Stewardship Council® certified paper.*

Orca Book Publishers gratefully acknowledges the support for its
publishing programs provided by the following agencies: the Government
of Canada through the Canada Book Fund and the Canada Council
for the Arts, and the Province of British Columbia through
the BC Arts Council and the Book Publishing Tax Credit.

Edited by Tanya Trafford
Cover photography by Shutterstock.com
Author photo by Bart Jackson

ORCA BOOK PUBLISHERS
www.orcabook.com

Printed and bound in Canada.

20 19 18 17 • 4 3 2 1

In memory of my mother, who gave me my love for history. And to our ancestors, who were irresistibly adventurous (if impractical) enough to fight on Charlie's side lo these four centuries ago.
—MJ

Down, too fast, into darkness. The chill air whipped at my face, jammed the 3-D glasses against my eyeballs.

I gripped the sides of the car. It wasn't the drop that scared me. I'd been on thrill rides before.

It was not being able to see.

The train wrenched to the left. Even safety-clamped to my seat I lurched sideways.

A loud, shrill scream rang out. Its echo was even more agonizing— a howling like the cries of the dead. I pressed my hands over my ears.

A huge green head blazed out of the darkness. It was a woman with snakes writhing from her scalp.

Her slithery head loomed larger, closer. The snakes lunged at me. Blood dripped from their fangs.

It was all a cartoon. I knew that.

All the same, I started sweating.

The woman opened her mouth. I braced for another loud, shrill—

Chapter One

Scre-e-e-e-am!

The train barreled straight at me. It was the train's piercing whistle that made the screaming noise.

The whistle shrieked at me now like an accusation. I was at the edge of the platform. I stood on the other side of the painted safety line, the one you weren't supposed to cross.

I had tried out the ride a few days earlier. I wasn't going on it a second time. The darkness, the screams, that cries-of-the-dead echo—once was enough.

Besides, this was another type of thrill—to miss getting hit by inches.

The gush of air from the speeding train felt good. We were in a two-month drought that showed no sign of breaking.

The white sun blazed on the metal shield of the approaching locomotive. From the shield's center, the woman with the snaky hair glared out.

Medusa. In Greek mythology, Athena, goddess of war, carried Medusa's head around to scare off enemies.

Yeah, I could see how that would work.

The train ride, called Medusa's Scream, was the new tourist attraction in British Columbia's Fraser Valley. The locomotive ran on autopilot. It wrenched nine open-air cars on a twisty, plunging ride through an old converted gold mine.

I was here to see the manager about a job. I was early. I could have waited in the lobby, but I was the restless type. More fun to pass the time standing almost in the path of a zooming train.

The ad had read *Cook needed at Medusa's Scream food truck. Summer position. Just starting out? No problem!*

Being in high school, I was more like *pre*-starting out. I'd gotten into cooking after Mom died. Dad didn't like cooking, and the taste of takeout lost its appeal after a while. So I threw on an apron.

Eventually I'd zeroed in on pie making. Not dessert pies. Savory pies that we could have for dinner. Meat, fish, veggie—you name it. I realized I could combine all the Canada Food Guide requirements under one roof— that is, one crust. The all-in-one meal.

And a great way to keep the dish-washing to a minimum.

I'd also discovered I enjoyed it. I liked trying out ingredients, seeing how they worked with each other. It was like being a combination of artist and mad scientist.

And now I needed to find a job. So here I was, waiting for an interview. I didn't seriously think I had a chance at the cook's job. More likely I'd get some part-time shifts flipping burgers at McDonald's. If I was lucky.

But anything was worth a try.

The train slowed. I got a look at the shield close up before the locomotive slid by. Medusa's mouth was set in midscream. Who could blame her with a hairdo like that?

In the myth, Medusa and her slithery scalp could turn people to stone.

But I wasn't worried about getting a stone makeover.

It was the guy jumping from the still-moving train who had me concerned.

He hit the platform awkwardly and crashed to the ground.

I ran up to him. He was about my age, dark-haired, pale and dripping with sweat.

I helped him stand. "Wow, not even waiting until the train stopped! The ride must have really got to you."

He pulled away, tried to stand on his own. Winced.

I caught him by the arm. "I'm calling an ambulance. You might have broken that ankle."

The train stopped. People started climbing out of the cars. Some were laughing. A few looked shell-shocked. Pressing a hand over her mouth, one woman staggered to the washroom.

The boy looked about ready to heave too. "I lost track of the time. I'm late for my job at the gift shop. Klopper's going to kill me."

Karl Klopper was the manager of Medusa's Scream. He was the one I'd come to see about the cook's job.

I took it Klopper wasn't the most easygoing of bosses.

I tried to calm the boy down. "Relax. Everyone's late sometimes."

He glanced around, eyes wide with fear. "Klopper's already mad at me for not catching the cat. I've tried. But it's too fast for me. It climbed up one of those trees."

He pointed to the willows by the ride's chain-link fence. The branches drooped with the heat.

"Is it Klopper's cat? Let him catch it," I said.

I couldn't imagine getting upset about a cat. But then I wasn't a cat person.

I started sneezing if they came near me. If I ever got a pet, it would be a dog.

The boy's mouth trembled. "You don't understand. *The cat knows too much.*"

This guy needed a vacation. Or a quieter workplace. Hearing that piercing whistle all day couldn't be good for nervous types. It had him imagining things. A cat that knew *anything*, let alone too much? Give me a break.

I kept supporting him. With my other hand I was holding a box with one of my pies inside.

I set the box on the ground. I pulled my cell phone from my back pocket. I started punching in 911.

He grabbed the phone from me. "No! Klopper doesn't want trouble. I can't lose this job. Nobody else will hire me. I'm too shy. I'm not a people person."

His fingers were shaking so badly, my phone slipped through them. It landed screen side down on the cement.

"I'm sorry," he bleated. He picked up the phone. He pulled a cloth from his jeans pocket. He wiped the now-cracked screen with it.

A gaunt old man marched out of the Medusa's Scream gift shop. He wore jeans and a white T-shirt decorated with Medusa's head.

The badge on his T-shirt read *Karl Klopper, Manager*.

The kid thrust the phone and the cloth into my hand. He hobbled out of sight, behind a green plastic sculpture of Medusa and her slithery buddies.

Klopper walked along the train, surveying each car. A routine safety check, I guessed. Possibly also a barf check.

He noticed me and scowled. "You're the one I saw on the security camera. You were standing on the other side of the safety line when the train came in. The sign over there says to stay *behind* the line. You risking your life, moron?"

I noticed the boy peeking out from behind the Medusa sculpture. Klopper's back was to him. The boy limped quickly into the gift shop.

I noticed something else. Past the train, in the shade of a willow tree.

A gray cat, so fluffy that its fur stood out in a cloud around it.

Neon signs blazed in my brain. *Danger. Major sneeze alert. Repeat—danger.*

The cat was watching Klopper. I didn't have to worry about it coming within sneeze range. It shot up the willow trunk and vanished behind the leaves.

The cat knows too much. Was this the cat the boy was after?

Klopper was still scowling at me. "You waiting for the next Ice Age? I don't need clowns hanging around Medusa's Scream. Now get out."

Chapter Two

I put on my best serious, responsible expression. "I'm Chase Simon, Mr. Klopper. I'm here about the cook's job."

Klopper snorted. "Well, you can chase yourself right out of here. I need someone who knows how to obey rules. A clown like you could get the safety inspectors after me. Get the place shut down."

He stomped off to the gift shop.

I realized I was still holding my phone and the boy's cloth. I started to stuff them in a back pocket.

Then I felt something in the cloth. A flat, rectangular shape.

I spread the cloth out on my palm. The shape I'd felt was a plastic card. Medusa and her slithery buddies stared up at me from the center.

I looked closer. In one corner tiny initials were scrawled—*LF*.

On the other side was a thick black line. The card was a passkey.

The boy would need it back. No problem. I'd give it to him.

For now I stuffed the card, cloth and phone in my back pocket. I picked up my pie box from the ground.

Karl Klopper had been right about me. I didn't obey rules all that well.

I had to convince him that I could.

I started after him.

I went into the gift shop. It was filled with Medusa's Scream souvenirs— mugs, masks, balloons, all imprinted with her snaky head. No surprise there.

What was surprising was the marmalade. Marmalade in a thrill-ride gift shop? But there it was, jars of it, gleaming orange, lemon, lime. There was even a glowing red jar.

I checked what flavor the red one was. Blood orange.

Maybe it tasted better than it sounded.

Auntie's Marmalade, locally made! read the label. A sweet-faced woman beamed out from a drawing underneath. I recognized her from around town.

By the counter, Klopper was ripping into the dark-haired boy.

"This place has to run like clock-work. You need to start at one. Can you not get that through your thick, brainless skull?"

"I...I'm sorry, sir. I didn't notice the time."

"There can be no slipups," Klopper raged through gritted teeth.

I kind of thought he'd made his point. "Uh, Mr. Klopper?"

Klopper whirled. Irritation flashed across his leathery face. "Didn't I just tell you to get lost?"

I walked over to him. I held up my pie box. I lifted the lid. The aroma of chicken-curry pie wafted out.

Klopper took a long whiff. His scowl melted. He let out a faint moan.

That's the way to get the best of someone. Use their sense of smell against them.

Klopper's office was through a door at the back of the gift shop. He gestured me to a seat in front of his desk.

On the desk a Medusa's Scream mug held pens, pencils and a plastic fork.

Grabbing the fork, the manager dug into my curry pie. "Slides right down," he mumbled. "Love it."

While he ate, he read my résumé.

There wasn't much to it. I was taking culinary arts in school. I'd sold pies to neighbors, donated some to a school fundraiser. The previous summer, I'd cleaned tables at a pizzeria.

Too restless to watch Klopper eat, I got up. I wandered around the office.

On the wall hung a portrait of a dark-haired man wearing a kilt. He clenched a bright-silver Medusa shield.

Obviously, the kilted guy was heavily into the Greek myths. Either that or snakes.

Kilt-guy glared out of the portrait at me. I could imagine his thoughts—*You got a problem with that?* His fierce, blazing eyes dared me to take a punch.

The plaque underneath read *Archie McBride, 1830–63, owner of the Medusa Mine.*

Everyone in town knew about Archie McBride. Archie had brought his family over from Scotland in 1858 during the Fraser River Gold Rush. Archie was certain he was going find gold in the Fraser, make his fortune.

So were 10,500 other prospectors.

Some succeeded. Most found a few specks of gold and left. Archie wasn't so lucky. He scraped together the last of his money and bought the Medusa Mine—then died when it collapsed on him.

Stories like Archie's didn't discourage fortune hunters, however, then or now. To this day, gold-hungry tourists came here to pan the Fraser.

In my town they stopped by Pete the Gold Panner's shop. They rented metal pans, sifters and magnets to draw gold nuggets from the silt.

Like there would ever be any gold nuggets.

All day they sat on the riverbank, dipping their pans in the water. My buddies and I would hoot with laughter watching them. "Hey, suckers! Made your fortune yet?"

Then Pete the Gold Panner would storm out to yell at us. "Good-fer-nothin' troublemakers!" That made us laugh too.

All the tourists got out of their visits were the bumper stickers they were dumb enough to buy from Pete: *Everyone glitters with gold fever.* They actually stuck them on their cars. Unbelievable.

Archie's great-great-grandniece still lived in town. I knew Sophie McBride from school. Her dad and mom had died a few years back. She lived with her aunt.

Sophie looked a bit like Archie, except for the blazing eyes. Sophie was the quiet, serious type, into studying.

Klopper had already gobbled up almost half of the family-size pie. He waved his plastic fork at the portrait. "The McBride family still owns the mine. It was just sitting here, unused. Tilly McBride had the idea of turning it into a thrill ride. She hired me to build the ride, get it going."

Tilly McBride was Sophie's aunt. Now I put it together—she was the *Auntie* in Auntie's Marmalade. The sweet-faced woman on the jar.

The manager was studying the top of my résumé. I'd drawn a pie with steam floating up. Underneath I'd printed *Simon the Pieman*.

Klopper grunted. "As in the nursery rhyme. *Simple Simon met a pieman.* Very funny."

He narrowed his bright-blue eyes at me. "So. You're funny and you make good pies. But a mere kid, running the Medusa's Scream food truck? I don't know. You'd have to fry up a lot of burgers and fries in a hurry. No slacking."

I followed his gaze out the window. A black truck was parked near the entrance. A large, grinning wooden snake stretched along the top.

The words *MEDUSA SCREAMS FOR FOOD* were painted in lurid green along the snake's side. Picnic tables surrounded the truck.

By the side of the truck, two metal posts stuck up from the ground. It was your typical food truck. The side could be lifted, then propped on the posts. Inside there would be a food counter, grill and mini-kitchen.

Klopper tossed my résumé aside. Obviously it hadn't bowled him over.

I'd also given him a sealed envelope. He reached for that.

It was a reference letter from my vice-principal. The VP, Mr. Torrance, had scrawled his signature across the flap. This was standard procedure, Torrance had explained. Otherwise an applicant might forge and substitute their own letter.

Klopper held the envelope toward me. He wasn't going to bother opening it. He was sending me on my way.

I pretended not to understand. I put on a cheerful grin.

With a sigh Klopper tore open the envelope. He took out the letter, unfolded it.

I wondered what Torrance had said about me. It couldn't be that bad. Torrance told me off a lot for clowning around.

On the other hand, when he did, he had trouble holding back a smile.

Klopper finished reading. He set the letter in front of me. "Any comments?"

I leaned over. I read what Torrance had said about me.

Chase Simon is a friendly, cheerful young man. But he has a reputation for acting out, for causing trouble.

I am not sure Chase is responsible enough for a summer job.

Chapter Three

I imagined shoving a pie right in Vice-Principal Torrance's face. One loaded with black pepper.

But I knew Torrance was being honest. Saying it like he saw it.

And I knew why. It was my buddies and me laughing at Pete the Gold Panner and his tourists. Word had got around.

I stood. No time like the present to get that McDonald's application in. "Thanks anyway for seeing me, Mr. Klopper," I said.

The old man studied me, his eyes thoughtful. "Sit down, Pieman. It takes more than a reference letter to make up Karl Klopper's mind."

I sat down again. *I am not sure Chase is responsible enough for a summer job.* The words were branded red and raw in my mind.

"Tell me why you like making pies," Klopper said.

I shrugged. I wasn't feeling all that sociable right now.

But Klopper was waiting for a reply. He was giving me a chance.

I spoke reluctantly. "My mom died a couple of years ago. She loved cooking. I guess hanging around the kitchen, getting into cooking, is my way of staying close to her. Of not being so lonely without her."

I shifted in my seat. I wasn't comfortable sharing personal stuff. Besides, I had the humiliation of Torrance's letter to burn off. I needed to go outside, jump on my bike and ride off my anger.

I picked up an eraser stamped with Medusa's head. I held my palm down, turned it up. The eraser wasn't there. I held my palm down again, turned it up. The eraser was back.

It was nothing to slide something up and down your sleeve. Cheap magic. It passed the time in class, got the girls giggling.

Well, not all the girls. Not the serious ones, like Sophie McBride.

Klopper was watching me.

I realized I was doing exactly what Torrance had said I would. I was clowning around.

I put the eraser back on the desk. I thought of my mother, surrounded by cookbooks. Scribbling notes in them about things she'd do, add, differently. She'd be smiling in delight, the tip of her tongue sticking out of the side of her mouth.

I imagined Michelangelo looking like that when he was sketching out the different parts of the Sistine Chapel ceiling. Pleased, excited, at what he was creating.

I said, "Mom liked planning multi-dish dinners. What appy would go with what main. What soup, cold or hot, thick or brothy, suited the weather. She was artistic about cooking. I try to be creative like she was—only in a more compact way."

The manager rubbed his chin. "Suppose I let you sell your pies here, Pieman. You could keep the profits from those. As long as you serve up our burgers and fries, coffee and pop too."

I stared. It sounded like he was offering me the job. But he couldn't be. Not after that letter.

Klopper gave a half smile. He was enjoying my bewilderment. "Once they finish riding the Scream, our passengers want refreshment. Nothing like a good scare to build up an appetite."

I still couldn't believe it, even when Klopper scribbled my initials, *CS*, on a passkey and handed it to me. My own employee passkey.

The manager had hired me in spite of Torrance's letter. And I could sell my pies.

I was too stunned to do more than mumble out a thank-you.

Klopper still had that half smile. "You didn't expect to get the job, Pieman? I'll tell you something. Sometimes it's the not-ideal candidates who work out best. They work the hardest and stay loyal. Know why?"

"Uhh…" My brain was still stuck back on *You're hired*.

Klopper leaned across his desk. His eyes bored into me. "Because the not-ideal candidates know that for once someone believes in them. Trusts them not to make waves."

I remembered how Klopper had ripped into the dark-haired boy. How he'd yelled at me for standing on the wrong side of the safety line.

I didn't care about being yelled at. I wasn't a wreck like that boy. Klopper was giving me a chance, and I wanted to take it.

But there was one thing I had to ask. "Will part of the job include catching your cat? I have allergies."

Klopper looked startled. Then he barked out a laugh. "It's not my cat.

It's some stray. I'm worried the train will run it over. If I get hold of the critter, I'll take it to the SPCA. Not something for you to worry about."

So that's why he'd put the boy on cat-catching detail. He was being humane.

In my mind a tiny voice argued, *The boy said the cat knew too much. What's that about?*

I ignored it. I wanted to sell my pies. I needed career breaks, not tiny voices.

Besides, the boy was the nervous type. Nervous types imagined things.

I told Klopper, "I'm going to live up to your expectations, sir. I'm going to work hard and be loyal."

I had to fill out some forms. Klopper went into the gift shop, leaving me alone in his office.

I heard a woman talking out there.

"I must buy some of Auntie's Marmalade. Look at this lady on the label. What a sweet face!"

Another woman replied, "I can't think about marmalade. That horrible echo from the scream is ringing in my ears. It won't go away. I may have to see a doctor."

Ah, yes. The cries-of-the-dead echo from deep in the mine. I felt sorry for her.

I finished with the forms and put them on Klopper's desk. I walked to the door.

Klopper had said I could start the next day. I would go home, cook up some pies.

The two women I'd overheard were standing beside the shelves of marmalade. One was massaging her ears. The other called out to the dark-haired boy, "Which flavor do you recommend?"

The boy gnawed his lower lip, thinking. Klopper was nearby, straightening a row of Medusa's Scream mugs.

The boy said nervously, "I don't actually like marmalade. It's too bitter."

I choked back a laugh. Some salesperson!

The woman gave him a withering glance. "This one looks interesting." She reached for the jar of the blood-orange marmalade.

"No!" snapped Klopper.

His face was purple with fury. He grabbed the jar from the woman. He thrust a jar of lime marmalade at her instead. "Here. Try this. On the house."

He threw the boy a murderous look. Then he stomped into his office.

I didn't get it. What was wrong with the blood-orange marmalade? Why didn't Klopper want the woman to buy it?

Chapter Four

The boy ripped open a package of Medusa's Scream serviettes. He didn't bother taking one or two out. He wiped his forehead with all of them.

Shrugging, the two women left with the freebie jar. Outside they put up umbrellas against the blazing sun.

Some kids sauntered in. They found souvenir plastic snakes with springs attached. The idea was to hold the springs while you threw the snakes. The snakes lunged. Then they bounced back on the springs, as if recoiling.

For me, plastic snakes would have time-limited appeal. As in, a few seconds. But the kids kept tossing the snakes at each other over and over again.

I walked over to the boy. He was even paler than before.

"What was wrong with the blood-orange marmalade?" I asked.

He jumped. His feet actually left the ground. The guy should be in high jump, not retail.

"It was off," he said hoarsely. He did his thing of glancing over his shoulder. "Past its sell-by date."

I took a jar of lemon marmalade from the shelf. I turned the jar around. The label on the back listed the contents—lemon peel and juice, sugar, water.

There was no sell-by date.

I thought about the jar of blood-orange marmalade. It had glowed a bright, rich red. It had looked okay to me. No mold and not watery.

The kids finally got bored with the plastic snakes. They trooped outside to wait for the next Medusa's Scream ride.

Some of the snakes had fallen to the floor. I helped the boy gather them up.

I wanted to ask him why Klopper would be so upset about a jar of marmalade. Then I remembered my promise. I was going to be a loyal employee. One who didn't make waves.

It wasn't up to me to ask questions.

I was about to leave but then remembered I had the boy's passkey. I fished in my back pocket, found it.

I waved the card at him. "Are you *LF*? You dropped this."

His eyes widened. Then his pale face lit up with a grin. "Hey, thanks! I didn't even know I'd dropped it."

He opened his mouth. I realized he wanted me to stick the card between his teeth, as his hands were full of plastic snakes.

I held off. "I'm Chase Simon," I said.

He stared at me, mouth still hanging. Then he realized what I was waiting for.

"I'm Lars Fry," he said.

I stuck the card in his mouth. He clamped his teeth tightly on it and started putting the plastic snakes back.

I walked outside. I pulled my cap low over my face against the blistering white sun.

I wondered how Lars stayed pale. He must use mega-strength sunblock.

At home I began planning my pie making. I figured people at a thrill ride would be into snack size. So I'd make three-and-a-half-inch pies.

I decided to make two dozen. I'd pack them in my cooler and attach it to the back of my bike. Then I'd bring them home again if no one bought any.

Sheesh. Somebody would buy *one*, wouldn't they?

I knew the problem I was up against. Everybody went for burgers. Why did people always go for the same old, same old?

I biked to the grocery store. I prowled the aisles. I had to figure out a savory pie that could compete with burgers.

Dad's favorite was steak-and-mushroom. The flavor would sound good to customers, sure. But then they'd see the bubbling patties, the golden fries, on the grill. The aroma of browning onions would close the deal.

The aroma…

Klopper had melted at the aroma of my chicken-curry pie. Aroma was the key.

I was going to make pies that sent waves of deliciousness up people's nostrils. The shock-and-awe strategy.

Dad chewed, swallowed—choked. His eyes swam with tears.

"You don't think you overdid the chili, son?"

I dipped a spoon into my first-ever chili-con-carne pie. It was rich, thick and, yeah, possibly nuclear on the chili.

"You think?" I asked through my own tears.

Dad blew his nose on a paper towel. "I get what you're trying to do. But maybe a pie that's less...hostile?"

I nodded. A less-hostile pie. Okay. *Think, Pieman.*

I did some running on the spot. I stretched my arms up and out. Physically, cooking was an odd fit for me. Cooks stayed in a limited space, a kitchen, for a long time. But I'd always been the restless type. I didn't like staying still, staying quiet.

Just ask Pete the Gold Panner.

The running on the spot got the blood flowing to my brain. The opposite to hostile would be…friendly. Welcoming. Comforting.

Comforting was cookies, cakes, sweet pies. Nah. Forget desserts. I was a main-course type of cook.

Could a solid main-course pie be comforting?

I'd been thinking shock and awe. I'd been thinking chili or pepper.

I shut my eyes. I ran spices through my head. Mentally I tasted them.

Cinnamon. *That* was comforting.

I surveyed the stuff on the counter. I could use cinnamon with the peas, the carrots, the kidney beans. But I needed something else. Something to hold the pie together.

Cinnamon and…

"I have to go shopping for squash," I told Dad.

I checked my back pockets for my wallet.

My wallet was in one pocket. The other had a cloth sticking out of it. I drew out the cloth, along with my phone and Medusa's Scream passkey.

Except that when I looked closer, it wasn't my passkey. It had the initials *LF*.

This was Lars's passkey. I had given him mine by mistake.

No biggie. One employee passkey was the same as another, right? Lars and I could switch passkeys the next day.

But when I biked to Medusa's Scream the next morning, Lars was gone.

Chapter Five

The new cashier was tidying up the gift shop. Straightening things, putting things in neat rows. Polishing the glass counter to a painfully bright shine.

She would be doing this. She was just the type.

I looked at her over the cooler of pies I was carrying. I never knew how to talk to ultra-serious people. So I made a joke. "Wow, Lars. Talk about an overnight transformation."

Sophie McBride tossed back her long chestnut hair. She didn't smile. Of course she didn't. "Mr. Klopper had to let Lars go. He asked me if I'd take the cashier job."

"Klopper *fired* Lars?" I remembered the jar of blood-orange marmalade, Klopper grabbing it, throwing a murderous look at Lars.

So the jar had been past its sell-by date. Big deal. Firing Lars over that seemed a bit extreme.

Sophie's face softened. Slightly. "Were you friends with Lars?"

I thought of Lars's smile when I gave him the passkey. He'd been so happy that someone was being nice to him.

"Yeah," I said. "Starting to be."

I set my cooler on the counter. Just for a moment, so I could take off my ballcap and stuff it in my back pocket.

In that moment I happened to look, really look, at Sophie McBride for the first time. I got the full, melting force of her brown eyes.

Even feeling bad about Lars, I was dazzled. I wanted to say something to impress her. Something suave and witty.

I never got the chance. The insides of my nostrils tingled. Oh *no*. The tingling built, turned fiery. I couldn't stop it. I exploded a gale-force sneeze straight at her.

"Ew, a snot spray. Thanks a lot, Chase." Sophie checked herself—for collateral damage, I guessed.

I swung around. The gray cat—make that gray cloud—was on the counter. He was slurping coffee out of a mug.

Sophie rushed to the cat and picked him up. "What a sweetie! Where did you come from? You shouldn't be drinking coffee. I'll get you some water."

I jammed my nose into the crook of my arm to stop a second sneeze. This put me into a weird pretzel shape as I clutched my cooler. Again, not suave.

I staggered out of the gift shop.

I put my pies in the truck's oven. I set the oven on low and left the door open. The aroma of squash and cinnamon floated out over the counter. People smiled and went, "Mmmmmm."

And ordered burgers and fries.

I wanted to shout, *Are you afraid to be different? Are you robots, programmed to hold only one food idea at a time?*

I knew my foul mood wasn't just about people's food choices. I was still bothered about Klopper firing Lars Fry over a jar of marmalade.

But I couldn't say anything. That was the deal I'd made with Klopper. No waves.

Finally, at lunchtime, a family of vegetarians bought four pies. I was so grateful I gave them an extra one to take home.

After lunch there was a lull. I was restless from being cooped up in the truck. I jumped out the back. I did cartwheels on the grass. I stood on my head.

A little boy walked up. "Why are you standing on your head?"

"I'm a restless pieman."

"What does *restless* mean?"

"It means I'm not happy about something that happened to a friend."

The boy stared at me solemnly. "You make pies?"

"Yeah."

"Apple pies?"

"Nope."

The boy got up, toddled away. I bent my knees and rolled forward. I stood up. I did some running on the spot.

The boy came back with a woman.

"Are you the restless pieman? My son Joey would like to try one of your pies."

I stopped running on the spot. I looked at Joey. He was obviously into sweet pies, not savory.

I wanted to sell my pies. But not under false pretenses.

"Joey wouldn't like them," I said.

Joey looked back at me. His face crumpled. He opened his mouth and let out a scream to rival Medusa's.

"A pie. Right away," I said.

I hopped back into the truck and then handed him a small squash pie through the side opening. I didn't think he'd eat it.

He gave me an I'll-show-you look. Then he crammed it back.

Other moms saw him. Their eyes widened at the sight of a kid eating something made mostly, aside from pie shell, of squash.

Joey's mom beamed. "My son has decided on a healthy lifestyle. I like to think"—she patted her hair—"it's because of the good parenting he's received."

I doubted it. I thought it was because I'd hesitated about letting Joey have a pie.

"CBEE News should do a story on this," Joey's mom was saying.

CBEE was our local TV station. I thought Joey's mom was a bit full of herself. CBEE News doing a piece on what a great parent she was?

She went on, "I'm so glad Medusa's Scream offers alternatives to burgers."

Yes. Finally someone had said it!

Time for a victory dance. I clenched my fists and raised them. I jumped from one foot to the other.

Joey's mom pointed at me and giggled. She told the other moms, "He's the 'restless pieman,' you know."

She bought a pie for herself. Other moms followed. Soon I was sold out.

I nodded wisely at the moms. "Nothing like a savory pie to get that cries-of-the-dead howling out of your mind."

"What cries-of-the-dead howling?" asked Joey's mom.

I stared at her. She and Joey had been on the ride just now. She had to have heard it. "The echo that the scream—the train whistle—makes in the mine."

"I didn't hear any echo."

She glanced at the other moms. They shook their heads. They hadn't heard it either.

I wanted to argue with them. But I was in business now. When you're in business, the customer is always right.

Then something took my mind off the cries-of-the-dead echo. Something that in its own way was just as scary.

A deadly tickling in my nostrils.

Chapter Six

Holding my nose, I whipped around.

I had a plate of cheese slices on the counter. The gray cat was gobbling them up.

"Hey! That's not cat food," I objected.

The cat looked up. He blinked his eyes at me. Then went back to eating.

"Seriously? You'll make yourself sick."

Kids were laughing. Moms were cooing about how cute the cat was.

I let him polish off the slices. I felt sorry for him. He ate like he was starving.

I was still holding my nose. But I couldn't run the food truck one-handed. I recalled seeing some papers clipped together, instructions for operating the grill. I rummaged in a drawer, found them.

I removed the metal clip. I clamped it on my nose. Now I was sneeze-proof.

People snapped my photo. They didn't know I was allergic. Obviously, they thought I would do anything for a laugh.

What the heck. I gave them a deep bow.

The cat prowled over to the sink. He waited for water to drip. When it did, he shot out his long pink tongue to catch it.

He was thirsty. Who wasn't in this heat? And he had all that fur to heft around.

I ran some water into a bowl and placed it in front of him. He slurped it back like he'd just dragged himself across a desert.

"Is that your cat, Pieman?" Joey's mom asked.

"Nothing to do with me."

Klopper had said I didn't have to worry about the cat. But now that I'd seen the sneeze machine up close, I did worry. He needed to be at the SPCA. In this heat, without water, he might die.

I petted him. He stretched his head back against my palm. How about that? Sneeze Machine liked me.

I put both arms around him. I could feel how thin he was under the cloud of fur.

"We're going to get you help, buddy," I said.

Sneeze Machine stiffened. He stared past me. He arched his back. He bared his teeth and hissed.

Why was this friendly cat so hostile all of a sudden?

I followed his gaze.

It was fixed on Karl Klopper.

The manager was marching toward us. He held a pillowcase open like a sack.

"Put him in here!" Klopper shouted.

Drop Sneeze Machine inside a *pillowcase*? That seemed kind of disrespectful to the Sneeze. Not to mention hot and claustrophobic.

On the other hand, Klopper would be taking Sneeze Machine to the SPCA. Getting him out of my hair.

More to the point, getting *his* hair away from *me*.

Klopper stomped closer. He wasn't just gripping the pillowcase. He was white-knuckling it.

Sneeze Machine let out a heart-breaking wail.

I told the Sneeze, "It's fine. Klopper's going to drive you to the SPCA. It's just down the Fraser River."

Then I thought about it. The river. Sneeze Machine in a pillowcase.

Klopper might not bother with the SPCA. He might stop his car by the Fraser. Hurl the bagged-up cat into the rushing water.

Nah. That was crazy. Klopper wouldn't drown the Sneeze.

Would he?

The manager was in front of the food truck. He held out the pillowcase.

I realized I was hugging the Sneeze

tightly—but he wasn't getting to me. *Right.*

I removed the metal clip.

Fireworks exploded inside my nostrils. I put Sneeze Machine on the floor. I blasted out a tornado-like sneeze.

Alarmed, parents, kids and Klopper retreated. I could have sworn the grass in front of the food truck bent backward.

Sneeze Machine bounded out of the food truck. He zoomed to the willow tree and shot up the trunk.

"Sorry," I said to Klopper. "Can't control my allergies."

Klopper bunched up the pillowcase in his fists. "Doesn't matter. He'll come back to the food truck eventually. I'll be watching for him. I'll get him tomorrow."

He stomped away.

Something about the cat really bothered him.

Pale, scared Lars appeared in my mind. He did his nervous glancing-around thing. Then he leaned forward and whispered, *The cat knows too much.*

I had to ask Lars what he meant. On my phone I looked up the Frys' number. I called it, asked for Lars.

A quavering female voice replied, "He's still at work."

"He has another job already?" I exclaimed. "Wow, that's great."

The voice grew impatient. "He has the same job. Who is this?"

The *same* job? I thought, puzzled. Lars must not have told his mom about getting fired.

Well, it wasn't my place to blab on him. "Sorry, I guess I'm confused. This is a buddy of his. Chase Simon. Please say hi for me," I said and hung up.

I had to forget about Lars and his cat theory. I needed to concentrate on what pies to make that night.

I shut the food truck down. I set my now-empty cooler on the grass. I did some cartwheels. For a grand finale I stood on my head.

Joey's mom would have said I was being restless. Fair enough. But restlessness cleared the mind. While standing on my head I was able to make an executive decision. I would bake more squash pies tonight.

I'd also try one of those fancy meat pies from Quebec. *Tourtières*, they were called. I had tried making one before. In my enthusiasm I had over-spiced it. I'd ended up slathering it with ketchup. Ketchup saves anything.

I stood up. I noticed the truck had a chalkboard attached to its passenger door. It must be for writing the daily specials on.

I picked up the piece of chalk on the blackboard's ledge. I wrote:

The Restless Pieman will return tomorrow.

I stood back and looked at the name. I liked The Restless Pieman better than Simon the Pieman. It was more interesting. It was more boss.

Maybe, just maybe, this was the start of something.

The train chugged slowly into the mine, with no screams. The whistle was turned off.

Klopper was taking the train for a safety check. He had told me he did this at the end of each day. He needed to make sure the train was running fine. He picked up stuff that had fallen from the fast-lurching train. Sunhats, sunglasses, even jewelry.

I walked over to the willow tree. I gazed up into its leaves. I had the metal clip ready to put on my nose.

"Hey, Sneeze," I called. "Come down. I need to get you to the SPCA."

In the still, dry heat no leaves stirred. But I knew he was up there. My nostrils were tingling.

I sighed. That was a cat for you. Useless. If you called a dog, it would break the sound barrier to get to you.

Through the lobby window I saw Sophie in the gift shop. I decided to apologize for sneezing at her. After all, we were co-workers.

And she did have those brown eyes.

When I got inside, Sophie was kneeling by the gift-shop safe. She had the door open. She was about to put envelopes of money inside, to the right of a passkey.

Frowning, she lifted it out. "Looks like someone's been chewing on this."

I looked over her shoulder. Sure enough, tooth marks dented both sides of the passkey.

She peered closer at it. "Hey, these initials are yours. *CS*. This is your passkey."

Of course. I had popped the passkey between Lars's teeth. His hands had been full of plastic snakes.

I said, "Lars and I got our passkeys mixed up. I saw him chomping on this when his hands were full. I meant to switch passkeys with him when I realized the mix-up, but then he got fired. He must have put this one—mine—in the safe before he left."

Sophie shook her head. "Klopper only keeps his spare passkey in the safe. It's different than employee passkeys. The manager's passkey opens everything."

I shrugged. "This is too much for my heat-addled brain, Sophie. Maybe Klopper chews on his passkey too, and that's why he got his mixed up with mine. People have all kinds of habits. Could be that chewing on passkeys helps him think."

The idea made even serious Sophie laugh. "You don't understand, Chase. Klopper wears dentures. He has problems keeping them in. He told me he only eats soft foods, the kind that don't need much chewing."

No wonder Klopper had been so pleased with my curry pie. *Slides right down. Love it.*

But that didn't explain why my passkey was in the safe.

Or why Klopper's spare passkey wasn't.

Chapter Seven

Through the window Sophie and I watched the train sliding up beside the platform. Klopper climbed out carrying a cardboard box.

He marched into the lobby, then through the gift shop. He nodded curtly at us. "Just locking up the lost-and-found stuff."

Sophie started to tell him about the tooth-marked passkey. Klopper waved her off. "Enough for today. I'm beat. Talk to me tomorrow."

He placed the box in his office. Then he locked the office door and marched out to his car.

Sneeze Machine crawled down the trunk of the willow tree. He saw Klopper's car disappear around a bend.

He raced along the train tracks and into the mine.

What would a cat want in a hot, stuffy old mine?

Sophie was watching him too. "The mine probably has rats. That's what your cat is after. He's hungry."

"He can't be. He just ate a bunch of cheese. It's something else."

Sophie put the tooth-marked passkey back in the safe along with the money. She closed and locked the door.

"Maybe your cat is the reincarnation of my great-great-granduncle. Archie McBride couldn't stay out of the mine either. He was sure everybody else was wrong and he was right, that somewhere, deep down, the mine held gold."

"Stubborn guy," I commented. "But the cat isn't mine. He makes me sneeze."

"With all that fur, of course he makes you sneeze. If you gave him a good brushing, a lot of it would come off."

I took out the metal clip. Pressing the hinges, I made the clip open and shut like a talking mouth. I made my voice high-pitched. "I'm Marty Metal-Clip. With me on your nose, you don't need to brush cats."

Sophie pursed her lips in disapproval. Hoisting her backpack onto one shoulder, she started going around the shop and lobby, turning off lights.

Okay, maybe it hadn't been the height of wit. I put Marty the talking clip back in my pocket. I followed Sophie. "So Archie was obsessed. He kept digging and hacking and drilling deeper into the mine. What made it collapse?"

Sophie looked out at the mine. "He and his crew hit soft earth. At that point they should have brought wood in, built a tunnel. But…" She shook her head. "They just kept going. And then it collapsed. It took days to dig out the bodies."

I thought of the fierce-eyed man in the portrait. Yeah, I could see Archie being too impatient to bother with safety rules.

I imagined soil and rocks crashing down on the men. The darkness as their lanterns went out. Their disbelief, then terror, as they couldn't move or breathe.

I remembered being on Medusa's Scream. The train plunging into darkness. The screaming whistle—and the echo it made. A howling like the cries of the dead. If I believed in ghosts, I would think the howls came from Archie and his crew.

I knew I should leave. I had groceries to buy, pies to make.

I also knew why I was hanging around. Sneeze Machine might reappear.

And face it, Pieman, I thought. You like being with Sophie.

I glanced out at the train parked by the platform. The late-afternoon sun burned the shield into orange. Medusa's snaky 'do seemed to be on fire.

"Why did Archie call it the Medusa Mine?" I asked. "Was he that into myths? Or snakes, or girls with problem hair?"

Sophie viewed me with exasperation. "Archie named the mine in honor of our Scottish rebel ancestors. In 1745 the

McBrides joined Bonnie Prince Charlie in fighting the English. Prince Charlie had a silver shield with Medusa carved on the front. He had extra shields made for his supporters. He gave one to us."

She followed my gaze to the shield on the train. "That's a tin copy of our shield. We keep the original silver one at home."

I tried to remember studying the Scottish rebellion in school. I couldn't. No surprise. I barely scraped by in history.

I could remember the words in a recipe. They turned into something you could look at, smell and taste. Long-ago dates and dead people's names, I had trouble with. They just stayed words.

But I liked the idea of charging at your enemies with a Medusa shield. That I could picture. That I could *feel*. "What happened to the rebels?"

"They won a great victory at a place called Prestonpans. But the English were too powerful. Eventually they overwhelmed the Scots. They rampaged through the country, burning the homes and crops of everyone who supported Prince Charlie. Left them with nothing."

Sophie gave a wry smile before continuing, "Aunt Tilly doesn't think much of the Bonnie Prince. She says his cause was hopeless and our ancestors were losers for following him."

I took out my phone. I googled Bonnie Prince Charlie. A blond, blue-eyed guy with a longish face appeared on the screen.

"How come they called him Bonnie? That's a girl's name."

"Shows how much you know," Sophie scoffed. "*Bonnie* is also a Scottish word for beautiful. Or, in the case of a man, handsome."

I studied Charlie some more. Yeah, I could see the ladies finding him bonnie.

But he was more than bonnie. He looked intelligent, thoughtful. He had a tough glint in his eyes. I could imagine his answer to Aunt Tilly: *How do you know a cause is hopeless if you don't try it?*

"I can see why your ancestors followed him," I said.

"Me too. But don't tell my aunt that!" Sophie blushed. "I don't mean to criticize Aunt Tilly. She's just very serious about life."

And she's made you serious too, I thought.

Aloud I said, "Yeah, well, I guess I'm the lost-cause type myself. I'm aiming to be a world-famous pie maker."

Sophie smiled. "I don't know if that's a lost cause. I bought one of your pies at the school fundraiser this spring. Steak-and-mushroom. Aunt Tilly and I really enjoyed it! And she is tough to please, even with her own cooking."

I glanced at the jars gleaming on the shelves. I thought of Klopper raging at Lars. "Was it your aunt's idea to get rid of the blood-orange marmalade? The jar I saw looked fine."

Sophie stared at me. "What are you talking about?"

"The marmalade. There wasn't any mold."

"I don't think you understand, Chase. There *is* no blood-orange marmalade. It isn't one of Aunt Tilly's flavors."

We stepped outside. After the air conditioning, the heat pressed on us like a smothering blanket.

"I saw the jar, Sophie. A lady wanted to buy it. Klopper grabbed it from her. It wasn't supposed to be on the shelf. I think that's why he fired Lars."

Sophie shook her head. "Klopper fired Lars because he kept slacking off.

People would come to the gift shop, but it wasn't open. Lars was just too nervous to deal with customers."

The nervous part sounded like Lars. The slacking off didn't. "The last thing Lars wanted to do was make Klopper mad," I said.

Sophie wiped the back of her hand across her forehead. "Well, Klopper didn't say anything about blood-orange marmalade. He wouldn't. Because there isn't any."

"Yeah. There is."

The heat wasn't helping our tempers. We walked to the bike rack in silence. She unlocked her bike. I kept going until I reached the shade of the willow tree. I set my cooler down. Then I stood on my head.

Sophie pushed her bike through the willow leaves. In the drought the leaves had turned yellow, like old, faded drapes.

"What are you *doing*, Chase Simon?"

"I'm waiting for Sneeze Machine to come out of the mine."

"He could be in there all night."

"Fine with me. I'll study the stars." I gave her an upside-down glare. "And by the way? I don't make things up."

"I didn't say you made things up. I said there is no blood-orange marmalade." For emphasis Sophie rang her bike bell.

She sighed. In a more reasonable voice she said, "You can ask Aunt Tilly tomorrow if you don't believe me. Every Thursday she comes in early, around seven, to restock the gift shop with fresh marmalade."

"Maybe I will," I said. "I know what I saw."

We heard something over by the mine. A scattering of pebbles. Sneeze Machine maybe.

I jumped up. I looked through the willow leaves.

Someone was exiting the mine. But it wasn't Sneeze Machine. I should have known. A cat wouldn't be that loud.

It was Lars Fry, hurrying out along the tracks.

Chapter Eight

Sophie's eyes blazed, not unlike Archie McBride's in that portrait. "What was Lars doing in the mine? There's nothing down there but special-effects props and train tracks."

I shrugged. I was as puzzled as she was.

"Whatever he's doing, he's trespassing," Sophie said.

I watched as Lars took a large black umbrella from his backpack. He opened the umbrella up against the sun.

Using a passkey, he opened the main gate. He hurried out.

We both watched the large black umbrella bob along the road and around the turn.

Sophie took out her cell phone. "I'm phoning Klopper."

"Don't. Please."

She hesitated.

"Let me look into this," I said. "Lars wouldn't risk Klopper's rage. If Lars was in the mine, he was supposed to be. Let me talk to him, find out what's going on."

She still looked doubtful.

I tried again. "Can you give me until tomorrow? Hey, I'll make you a *tourtière*. Eet weel be *très* delicious, mademoiselle."

Sophie did her disapproving pursed-lips thing. But the corners of her eyes were crinkling. I realized something. The pursed-lips thing wasn't disapproving. It was what she did when she was trying not to smile.

I grinned at her. It was too much to think that she might actually like me. No.

But she didn't mind me.

"That was a *terrible* French accent, Chase," Sophie said. She moved her bike away from the willow trunk. "You biking into town?" she asked.

I wanted to go with her. I wanted to spend more time with serious Sophie McBride. Who maybe wasn't so serious all the time.

As a bike buddy, she would be a safety hazard, with those distracting brown eyes. But I thought I could avoid smashing into stop signs.

Instead I leaned against the tree. "I'm going to wait here for a while. See if Sneeze Machine comes out. Get him to the SPCA, if I can. Then I'll drop by Lars's place."

She nodded. She biked to the gate. Opening it, she called back, "Nobody can go into the mine without permission. No exceptions. You'll tell Lars that?"

I stepped out from the willow leaves and gave her a reassuring wave. "Yeah, I'll make that clear."

She smiled and waved back. I watched her bike away. Her long chestnut hair flew behind her like a banner.

Then I headed straight into the Medusa Mine.

I didn't like deceiving Sophie. But I had to find Sneeze Machine. He was a cat. He didn't get it about rules.

What if he fell asleep on the tracks? The first train of the morning could run him over.

Friends don't let friends become roadkill.

I was walking along the railway ties. I almost slipped. I had to be careful. One misstep between the ties, and I could twist my ankle.

I was about a hundred yards in. It was getting darker. The ties were harder to see. I glanced back. The mine entrance was now a small, white, upside-down U.

As if to make up for the gloom, my imagination flashed an image at me. Archie McBride, scowling. *Gold, I tell you. Nobody believes me. But I know it's here.*

I took out my phone. I switched the light on. I kept stepping from tie to tie.

I came to the mineshaft. This was where the train took its steep plunge. I stared down. My phone light hardly pierced the blackness.

Using the ties as a ladder, I'd have to climb down.

But with this feeble phone light?

There had to be a light switch around here somewhere.

I aimed my phone light up and down the craggy mine walls. I almost missed it, the black switch blending in with the shadows.

I flipped it. The walls and the shaft lit up. Darkness made the ride scary, mysterious. In plain light the mine was shabby gray, the tracks jutting across its dirt floor like scars.

"Hey, Sneeze!" I called. "Be a pal. Come on out so I don't have to try to find you."

My voice bounced around the walls of the drop. I had probably scared Sneeze Machine into permanent hiding. *Good one, Pieman.*

I started climbing down the drop. It was maybe fifty feet down, twenty wide.

I had thought of the ties as being like a ladder. But a real ladder has rungs with air on both sides. The ties were attached to the wall. The top of each tie was maybe three inches wide. I had to feel carefully for a toehold.

It was a long, tense descent.

When I reached bottom I shook off the tension with some running on the spot. I surveyed the tunnel stretching to my left.

Hanging down the middle was a blank projection screen.

During the ride you didn't see the screen. You saw Medusa's huge, snaky head. I craned my neck back. A projector hung directly overhead. The only snaky thing now was the wires coming out of it.

"Sneeze Machine?" I called softly. I walked along the ties. I kept waiting for my nostrils to start tingling.

I passed under the screen. I remembered Medusa and her hissy buddies lunging, blood dripping from their fangs.

And the screaming whistle with its cries-of-the-dead echo.

No Medusa now. No snakes. No screaming whistle.

Weird thing though.

The cries-of-the-dead echo still howled down the tunnel.

Chapter Nine

On the ride my brain had done the logical thing. It had matched the howling to the scream. It had taken the howling for an echo.

But the howling wasn't an echo. It wasn't even howling.

It was meowing.

It was Sneeze Machine calling for help. The tunnel picked up his meows and gave them that cries-of-the-dead effect.

I kept walking along, watching for him. Now I got why some riders heard the howling and some didn't. It depended on whether the Sneeze was down here.

I wondered why he came into the mine if it scared him so much. Crazy cat.

I erupted in a massive sneeze. The echoes were like bomb blasts. I clamped the clip over my nose to stop a second explosion. I didn't want to trigger another mine collapse.

I did a slow three-sixty. No sign of Sneeze Machine.

But nostrils don't lie, I thought. The nose knows.

"Sneeze?"

A whimpering answered me. The Sneeze was tired, meowed out.

He was also close by. Not in the tunnel though. The whimpers were coming from behind the wall.

I stepped up to the gray rock. How had he gotten behind that? Crazy, crazy cat.

I leaned forward, pressed my hands against the wall. I pushed all my weight into my palms. I did some sideways push-ups. Restless people don't like enclosed spaces.

My restlessness kept me in pretty good shape. That happens when you can't stay still for long. I knew I was pretty fit.

Even so, I was surprised when the rock buckled under my palms.

I stood back, startled.

Where my palms had been there were now two dents in the rock.

There was a chance, a spaghetti-thin chance, I would become a superchef one day. But a superhero? I had no illusions about that.

This could not be rock.

I ran my hands over the surface. It was thick plastic.

What I had dented with my super strength was a bumpy gray cover, designed to blend in with the rock. To hide an opening.

Maybe this was some secret man cave of Klopper's.

From the other side, Sneeze Machine meowed louder. He scratched at the plastic.

I leaned close again, squinted. I made out the line where plastic met rock. It ran up and around in a jagged door shape.

I pushed sideways. A section of plastic in the middle slid to the left. Now I was looking at a rectangular black sensor like the ones at the gate and office doors.

The only way in was to punch through the plastic. That or shoulder-ram it. Either way, there was going to be some serious property damage. I could just imagine Klopper's wrath.

I wondered if they let you practice cooking in reform school.

Sneeze was only a cat, I reminded myself. All this trouble for a cloud of fur.

Then I remembered how thin Sneeze had felt under that fur. How he'd rested the back of his head against my palm. Liking me, trusting me.

There was no getting around it. The cat had got to me.

I flexed my fists. I thought of the manager's all-powerful passkey. The one Sophie had talked about. If only I had it, the passkey that opened everything. I only had Lars's employee passkey.

I drew back my fist, ready for the first punch. I shut my eyes. For Sneeze

Machine's sake I'd do this. But I couldn't watch.

A vision swam against my eyelids. Lars's happy smile as I put his passkey between his teeth. As he clamped down on it.

I opened my eyes. Stared hard at the door.

Lars had been down here. Had he gone through the door? I couldn't think why else he'd be in the mine.

If so, he couldn't have used my passkey to get in. It wouldn't work.

I pictured him swiping my passkey against the sensor. Wondering why the door didn't budge.

He would have looked closer at the passkey, seen my initials.

Lars knew the combination to the safe. He could have gone back out, sneaked into the office, swapped my passkey for the manager's spare one.

But it wasn't the swapping out that bothered me. It was Lars coming down here in the first place, confident his own passkey would work.

Why would Lars have a passkey to Klopper's man cave? Employee passkeys were only supposed to open the front gate.

From my back pocket I pulled out Lars's passkey. I felt like I was in a dream. It didn't make sense that this passkey would work.

And yet...

When I swiped the passkey, the red light turned green. The door swung open.

Cooing like a pigeon, Sneeze Machine wrapped himself around my legs. I picked him up. Time to vacate the man cave.

But not before I had a quick look around. One peek wouldn't hurt.

The door opened to a massive gray rock. A short ladder leaned against it. I walked over and beamed my phone light down.

Something ahead reflected the light back to me.

I was looking at a stream. It must be an underground tributary of the Fraser. How about that? The old river still had its surprises.

At last I understood why Sneeze Machine came into the mine. It had been in front of me all the time, as blazingly obvious as the white, burning sun.

Sneeze Machine came into the mine for water.

At first he had probably come in for the shade. Then, smelling dampness, he'd gone exploring.

I looked farther along the stream. I saw a metal pan. Beside it, a large bucket held a shovel, bowls and magnet.

I understood something else at last too—the reason Klopper was keeping his man cave a secret.

He was panning for gold.

Chapter Ten

There's nothing down there but special-effects props and train tracks.

So Sophie thought. So she and her aunt believed.

Crafty Karl was running his own little gold-panning operation down here—without telling them.

Tilly McBride had put Klopper in charge of building the ride. No one had been in the Medusa Mine for years. I bet Klopper had discovered the stream—and decided to keep the gold for himself.

Because deep down, like the bumper stickers said, everyone glitters with gold fever. Everyone is greedy.

Problem was, Klopper was the ride's manager. He had to be seen above ground.

So he must have sent Lars down. That's why Lars hadn't been around the gift shop in the mornings.

I also got why Lars stayed so pale in this summer of nonstop sun. Hours a day in a man cave will do that to you.

But how much gold were we talking about? I thought of the tourists panning for gold in town. They got excited if the Fraser yielded a single speck. This whole area had dried up long ago.

Hadn't it?

I set Sneeze Machine on the rock. I climbed down the ladder, knelt by the stream. The softly flowing water lapped against the silt of the bank. I reached for the pan.

My buddies and I had laughed at the gold-hunting tourists. But we had also watched them. I knew what to do.

I scooped enough silt and water to fill a third of the pan. I shook the mixture in a circular motion. It was like shaking dough and flour when making a pizza crust.

Like cooking, it took patience. The idea was to dislodge the lighter stuff—the sand, soil and clay—so that it rose to the top. Gold was heavy. If there was any, it would stay at the bottom of the pan.

I kept shaking the pan, sloshing out water and silt. I considered grabbing the magnet from the nearby bucket. I could speed things up by using the magnet to draw the black sand off.

It turned out I didn't have to.

In the bottom of the pan, several gold nuggets gleamed up at me.

The stream gurgled, as if chuckling. It was a young stream, just forming and growing. In Archie's time it hadn't pushed gold-laden silt through the rocks. It hadn't existed.

But Archie's instinct had been right. One day his mine would pay off.

Klopper's deal with Tilly McBride had been to build the ride, get it up and going. He'd bragged about that when he hired me.

I rolled the gold nuggets around in the pan thoughtfully. Before crafty Karl left, he wanted to get as much gold out as possible. I was guessing Klopper only pretended to fire Lars. He decided to keep Lars working down here all day.

Sneeze Machine jumped down to the stream for an H_2O refill. Then he walked over to me and wound around my ankles.

I set the pan down and picked him up. I nuzzled my metal-clipped nose into his furry head. "Here's what I think happened. You found the stream. If Klopper or Lars showed up, you hid.

"Sometimes they shut the door. You were stuck in here. You didn't like that, so, like any self-respecting cat, you howled your lungs out. You gave Medusa's Scream an echo.

"Klopper couldn't have some rider figuring out that the yowling was a cat, not an echo. That's why he was so desperate to bag you up for the SPCA, or more likely…"

Or more likely toss you in the Fraser River on his way home.

Sneeze Machine was studying me. If he guessed my thoughts, he took it calmly.

I glanced back at the man-cave door. We needed to get out of here. Klopper could show up for some nighttime panning.

But the cat had me curious. Maybe cats did that to you. I wanted to see what else was down here.

I walked along the bank. I aimed my phone light at my feet to make sure I didn't fall in. You never knew. The stream might take a sudden twist.

Not able to see what was directly ahead of me, I walked right into what luckily wasn't a rock wall.

I wrenched the heavy canvas curtain aside. I was in a small work/storage space.

A table held a row of orange industrial lanterns. I switched one on. Way better than my phone!

Tilly McBride smiled up at me from a stack of *Auntie's Marmalade* labels. I picked one up, squinted at it. Under Auntie's face the name of the flavor had been whited out.

The table also held a bottle of liquid paper and a black felt-tipped pen.

What were Klopper and Lars up to in here?

I shifted the lantern. To the left was a bookcase filled with jars of marmalade.

The jars didn't have labels on them yet. But I recognized the glowing red color.

Blood orange.

Chapter Eleven

Lars opened his front door a crack. He squished his face into the space and whispered, "I can't talk to you about the gold. It's a secret."

"Yeah, so secret Klopper hasn't told the McBrides. He's keeping it for himself. He's *stealing*."

I'd spoken louder than I intended. The thought of crafty Karl deceiving

Sophie and her sweet-faced auntie set my blood on broil.

I was carrying Sneeze Machine in my backpack, which I was wearing on my front like a baby carrier. At the sound of my voice the Sneeze woke up. He looked at Lars, yawned and went back to sleep.

I had something else in the bag too. A jar of blood-orange marmalade to show Sophie. Besides stealing gold, Klopper and Lars seemed to have their own marmalade side business going on. Whatever they were up to, we would find out about it.

A woman appeared behind Lars. In the quavery voice I remembered from the phone, she demanded, "Who is this boy, Lars? And why does he have a metal clip on his nose? Is this some punk thing?"

Lars's eyes widened. "I'll talk to you later, Chase! Please don't do anything until then!"

He shut the door.

I glared at it. I knew I should go to the McBrides, to the police. But I liked scaredy-cat Lars. I wanted to hear what he had to say before I did anything.

In the same loud voice I said, "Okay. But *later* better be *soon*."

"Hold still, Sneeze." I cut off another massive tuft of fur.

By the time I had biked the Sneeze to the SPCA, it was closed. A sign on the door gave a number for emergencies. This wasn't an emergency. I would just keep Sneeze Machine overnight at my place.

We were on the back doorstep. Gray fur was heaped around us. At the slightest breeze clumps of it floated and rolled around the yard. It looked like we'd had an attack of volcanic ash.

I scissored off another hunk of matted fur. I held Sneeze Machine away from me so I could admire my handi-work. "Wow, Sneeze. You have a neck! Who knew?"

Dad came around the side of the house with bags from the grocery store. "I bought litter and cat food," he began.

Then he noticed Sneeze Machine. "Uhhh…"

I beamed. "Good cut, huh? If the pie career doesn't work out, I might take up cat grooming."

Dad kneeled beside the Sneeze. "He looks kind of…patchy."

"I'm *ventilating* him."

The Sneeze sniffed at the grocery bags. He knew there was food inside.

"Now for the big test," I said.

I removed the metal clip from my nose.

My nostrils tickled, but just faintly. I let out a mild sneeze. Nothing like my megatonic ones.

We were making progress.

Dad and the Sneeze chill-axed on the sofa, watching a baseball game.

I shut the kitchen door. To cook, I needed to stabilize my nostrils. I needed to be able to smell.

Now for operation *tourtière*. I was determined to get it right this time.

I switched the stove on. I started browning the ground pork and beef, along with garlic, onion and a bunch of spices.

I inhaled the aroma. Yum. And yet— too goody-two-shoes. This mixture needed a bit of the devil in it.

I grabbed a bottle of curry powder from the shelf. I paused. Should I or shouldn't I? Once I did this, there was no going back.

I took the plunge. I added the curry.

I sniffed again. Oh, man. This *tourtière* was going to be wicked.

There was a nervous knocking at the window. I looked up and saw Lars's nose flattened against the pane.

I wrenched the window open. He jumped back.

"Can't you go to the front door like a normal person?" I demanded.

"I did go to the front. But I saw your dad through the living-room window with a weird creature beside him. Half skunk, half weasel. I wasn't sure it was safe to go in."

Yet another person failing to appreciate my hairdressing skills.

I got right to the point. "I discovered Klopper's man cave. Is he cutting you in on the profits?"

"Of course not! He just pays me a salary." Lars's mouth trembled. "I applied for so many summer jobs, Chase. I tried everywhere in town. Klopper was the only one who would hire me. I promised to keep the gold panning a secret. I owe him."

I remembered the vice-principal's reference letter. *I am not sure Chase*

Simon is responsible enough for a summer job. Klopper had read it and hired me anyway. Now I understood why.

Klopper wanted employees who would have trouble getting jobs elsewhere. Who would be grateful and keep quiet about anything unusual.

And here I had thought Klopper was being decent, giving me a break.

I turned back to the stove and stirred the *tourtière* mixture so hard that chunks of meat, garlic and onion flew out.

I took a deep breath to calm down. "Tomorrow's the day Tilly McBride goes in early to restock the marmalade. I'm going to get there early too. I'm going to tell her about the gold. Come with me."

"We can't! Klopper will be furious!"

I reached through the window to give Lars a friendly punch on the shoulder. "We'll both tell her what crafty Karl is up to. You know what? Tilly will respect us for letting her know. I bet she'll give us great references. We'll find other jobs."

I wasn't messing with Lars. I was picturing that smiling face on the marmalade label. I knew Sophie's aunt would stand by us.

A burning smell invaded my nostrils. The meat! *Noooo!*

I quickly switched the heat off and shifted the pan to another element. Once again I had screwed up *tourtière*.

Lars thought I was scowling because of him. "See you, Chase," he bleated— and ran off.

I'd screwed that up too. I hadn't convinced him to go with me to see Tilly McBride.

The meat mixture wasn't that burned. It would make an okay pie, but not one I could sell. Dad and I could have it tonight. I would add some green beans to it, maybe some corn.

I glanced around for the ketchup bottle. Ketchup, the all-purpose food saver.

I spotted my backpack. After lifting Sneeze Machine out, I had left it on a kitchen chair. Forget ketchup, I thought. Why not mix in some blood-orange marmalade? I bet it would be tasty.

I pulled the jar out, twisted the lid off. Turning the jar upside down, I spooned marmalade into the mixture.

Clunk, clunk!

Gold nuggets fell into the pan.

Chapter Twelve

Dad came into the kitchen for a between-innings beer. He saw the gold nuggets floating in the meat mixture.

"I hope you're planning to charge extra for this pie," he said.

I hadn't yet told him about finding Klopper's man cave. I'd wanted to wait to talk to Lars, hear his side of things first.

Now I did tell Dad. I explained about

going down into the mine for the Sneeze and finding a gold-filled stream.

I showed Dad the jar. "Sophie's aunt doesn't make a blood-orange flavor of marmalade. I'm guessing Klopper buys a cheap brand. He must hide the gold inside and then slap on *Auntie's Marmalade* labels."

Now I understood why the blood-orange marmalade I'd seen in the gift shop had shone in the jar. Gold gave it that extra glow.

Dad was frowning. "Why doesn't Klopper just carry the gold out in a bag?"

I shrugged. "Crafty Karl is playing it safe. If anyone finds him with marmalade jars, they won't be interested. It's gold that gets people excited."

Early the next morning I loaded my fresh pies into the cooler—squash, chicken-curry, steak-and-mushroom.

I added an extra pie shell and crust. In the food truck I would mix up a ground beef, cheese and onion pie. Feel-good food to give Sophie and her aunt. They would need some comfort after I told them what Klopper was up to.

For the fiftieth time I promised Dad I would call the police the minute Klopper showed up.

When I reached Medusa's Scream, the parking lot was empty. I was the first one here.

I unloaded all my pies into the food-truck fridge.

Tires scraped on the gravel. A sweet-faced woman in an ancient gray Volvo drove into the lot. Spotting me, Tilly McBride gave a friendly smile. Right away I felt better. Everything was going to be okay.

She started lifting a box from the trunk of her car. On her pointy high heels, she wobbled under the box's weight.

I went over to her. "I'm Chase Simon, Miss McBride. Here, I'll carry that box for you."

Her eyes twinkled. "Sophie told me about you. The Restless Pieman. We're lucky to have you running our food truck. And please call me Auntie. Most people do!"

I wanted to blurt out my story. Get it over with. But maybe not out here. Klopper might drive up at any moment.

I clamped my lips together to stop them from flapping.

I set the box on the gift-shop counter. Auntie unpacked the new jars of marmalade and set them on the shelves.

The wait was killing me. I considered doing a headstand. That always burned off some restless energy.

Nah. The gift shop had too many breakables. If I fell sideways I might upset that display of porcelain Medusa mugs. Or send the plastic snakes flying.

Auntie saw me eyeing the snakes. She shuddered. "The way those things leap from their springs! Enough to give you nightmares."

Uh-oh. Maybe she was the delicate type. Maybe I should get her to sit down before I broke the news.

"Thank you for carrying the box," she said sweetly.

"You're...you're..."

You're welcome, I was trying to say. What came out was, "You're the owner of a gold-bearing stream!"

Auntie marched into the mine. "I can't believe it!" she kept saying.

For someone in high heels, she sure moved fast. She was jumping from one railroad tie to the next.

I had to hurry to keep up. I wondered if she had gone into some kind of shock. "Are you okay, ma'am?"

She paused, smiled reassuringly. "You're an impressive young man, Chase. Karl Klopper thought he was being so clever, and yet you found him out. Imagine hiding gold in blood-orange marmalade! Well, we'll put a stop to Klopper and his gold-glowing jars. Now show me how you climbed down to discover his man cave."

We were a long way in, almost at the shaft.

"Uh…shouldn't we call the police first?"

Auntie took a cell phone from her dress pocket. "Smart boy! Of course. Just show me where you climbed down. The police will want every detail."

"Okay," I said. I walked ahead. I reached the edge of the shaft. I was standing on the last tie before the tracks plunged.

I needed a light. I felt for my own cell phone and realized I'd left it in my bag back at the food truck.

I would have to find the light switch.

Light, I thought. What did that remind me of?

Sunshine. Stars. Gleaming gold.

Gold that made blood-orange marmalade glow.

Auntie had just said, *We'll put a stop to Klopper and his gold-glowing jars.*

How did she know the jars glowed?

I turned to ask her.

I never got the words out. Because she was running straight at me, arms outstretched, palms up.

And she wasn't wearing a sweet smile either.

Chapter Thirteen

Auntie intended to send me on a no-return *splat!* to the bottom of the mine.

I ducked. But in trying to avoid those pushing hands, my right foot slid off the tie. I fell. From the ribs down I was now dangling over the edge.

The light-as-air feeling was not a good one.

I grabbed hold of the rails. I tried to pull myself up.

Auntie let out an angry squeal. She jabbed a pointy high heel into my left hand.

Ow. Talk about bringing in the heavy artillery.

She lifted her foot for round two. I grabbed her ankle. Balanced on her other foot, she twisted this way and that, trying to escape. We could have been contestants on *Dancing with the Stars*.

I shouted, "You *knew* about the gold? What's the big secret? It's your gold mine—yours and Sophie's!"

Auntie panted, "The property belongs to Sophie and me, yes. *But not the gold*. Pete the Gold Panner owns the claim on any gold found here."

I was so surprised, I almost let go of her ankle. Pete, with his tourist-trap panning equipment and cheesy bumper stickers?

Auntie stopped struggling. She rested on her free leg like a flamingo. "During the gold rush, Pete's ancestors staked dozens of claims with the government. Pete still owns the claims. That's why he's allowed to charge tourists to pan for gold in town.

"In 1896 Archie McBride staked a claim on this property. But when he died, he left debts. The McBrides were too proud to sell the land. But they were happy to sell Archie's claim to Pete's family. They were so sure the mine held no gold."

Auntie's voice turned whiny. "I've been a good aunt to Sophie. When her parents died I moved here and looked after her. But now, with the gold, I have a chance to live my own life—to break free of this small town! Oh, I'll hire a housekeeper to stay with Sophie. She's a good kid. She'll be fine!"

I needed Auntie to keep blabbing. If she got into full rant mode, I might be able to let go of her ankle and pull myself up with both hands.

"See, Pieman," she said with a frown, "*I* found the stream. *I* deserve to benefit from the gold.

"I made a deal with Klopper. He gets the gold out, I sell it and cut him in. Lots of money for both of us."

She wagged her finger at me as if I were a naughty kid not eating my broccoli. "Then you come along snooping! If you tell people about the mine, the gold will be Pete's. But I need it. It will give me all the things I never had. Jewelry. Clothes. Travel."

Then—

Auntie wrenched her foot free. Now my left hand held only her shoe. Meanwhile, I was still hanging on to the rail with just my right hand.

Auntie let out a triumphant cackle. She removed her other pointy-heeled shoe and held it high. "I can't let you get in my way. You do understand, don't you?"

"Actually, no..."

"Pieman, you are cooked." She aimed the spiky heel at my right hand.

I couldn't watch. I shut my eyes. "Noooo!" I yelled.

But the heel never found its target.

I opened my eyes. Lars had hold of Auntie. She was wriggling, kicking at him, but he wasn't letting go. He was stronger than he looked.

I tossed Auntie's shoe aside. I clamped my left hand onto the rail and with both hands pulled myself up.

I stood. I savored the feeling of solid ground under my feet.

Lars let go of Auntie and skittered over to me.

There wasn't a lot she could do facing two of us. She glared, panting. She jabbed a forefinger at Lars.

"*You!* Klopper told me you would be no trouble at all. A loser. A nothing."

Lars gulped. He opened his mouth. A frightened croak came out.

"This guy?" I said. "He's big, bad trouble. The worst kind."

Auntie scowled. "If you two say anything about this, I will deny it. I will say I knew nothing of the gold. You and Klopper were stealing what belongs to Pete the Gold Panner. I'll see that you end up in reform school. Both of you."

Her eyes narrowed craftily at Lars. "Reform schools are full of bullies. Just imagine what they'd do to a 'fraidy boy like you."

Lars let out a whimper.

Auntie hunted for her shoes and shoved her feet into them. She faced us again. Her breathing was more even. Now she was smiling and twinkly-eyed, like the face on the marmalade jars.

She tick-tocked a forefinger in front of Lars's terrified eyes. "Just remember. It's not nice to fool with Auntie."

She walked briskly out of the mine.

There was a *thunk* beside me.

Lars had fainted.

Chapter Fourteen

I got Lars to the food truck. I gave him a bottle of water. He glugged it back too fast and started coughing.

I clapped him on the back. "I'm proud of you, buddy. And I mean it about being my buddy. You saved me back there. Like it or not, you've got a pal for life."

Lars managed a pleased, if weak, grin. "Up until this morning, my philosophy was give in to your fears. They're good for you."

I laughed. "If you were that scared, you wouldn't have shown up early. You decided to stand by me and tell Auntie the truth, didn't you?"

A shy smile flashed across Lars's face. "But I'm not like you. You have too much personality to get scared."

"Oh yeah?" I showed him my hands. They were still shaking.

From across the parking lot I heard, "Hey, Pieman!"

We turned and saw a news van with a huge bee logo on the side. Two women were walking to the gate. One lugged a camera and black duffel bag. The other held a microphone.

The woman with the microphone waved at me.

It was Joey's mom.

Joey's mom in TV mode, that is. Her hair was piled up on her head. She wore a pink business suit. Powder caked her face, and lipstick made a red gash of her mouth.

"I *told* you I could get CBEE News to do a story," she beamed as I opened the gate.

She gave me her business card. *Penny Cutler, Reporter, CBEE News.* "I'm going to make you famous, Pieman."

"That's..." Amazing, actually. A dream come true. Just the break I needed. For an instant I forgot the life-or-death struggle I'd just been through. I grinned like an idiot.

Joey's mom tucked her arm through mine. She led me over to the food truck. "I wanted to get here before the park opens. That way we can prep for the interview. You can plan what you'd like to say—how you got into pie making, who inspired you, why you're so entertaining!"

The camerawoman was puffing to keep up. When she reached the truck she dumped her stuff on the ground. She grabbed the water bottle I'd given to Lars and knocked back the rest of it.

After a loud belch she said, "Yeah, let's prep. In TV, timing is everything."

"Timing. Yeah," I said uneasily.

I was thinking of Auntie. Her car was still in the lot. She must be in the office.

Dreams-come-true would have to wait. Auntie was running an illegal gold-panning operation. She had also tried to shove me down a mineshaft.

I couldn't let her get away. I needed to phone the police.

I was reaching into my backpack for my phone when Sophie ran up.

"CBEE News! This is so exciting, Chase!"

She spotted Lars. She whispered, "Hey, did you find out why he was trespassing in the mine?"

I hesitated. Penny was hovering. Her smile was growing impatient. She wanted to "prep" me.

I couldn't blurt out to Sophie that her aunt was a gold thief. Not with a TV reporter listening.

I pulled Sophie aside. I looked straight into her eyes. "You have to promise me something. Cross your heart and hope to—"

I choked on the word. I couldn't quite say the word *die*, not after my recent adventure.

Sophie thought I was setting up one of my jokes. She started to laugh.

Then she saw how miserable I looked. "What is it, Chase?"

Over her shoulder I saw Auntie leave the office. She was carrying the box she had brought in earlier, full of jars of fresh marmalade.

In theory she had set those new jars out in the shop. The box should now be empty. But Auntie was gripping it, staggering under its weight.

I was betting the box was full again. With value-added marmalade.

This must be the routine Auntie had worked out with Klopper. Once a week she showed up early to Medusa's Scream. She swapped her jars for the ones he and Lars had packed with blood-orange marmalade and nuggets of gold.

I had to stop Auntie before she got away with the latest haul.

I grabbed hold of Sophie's hands. "This is what you have to promise. That you will not be mad at me forever. Maybe for a month. Two months. But not forever."

"But I'm not mad at you *now*! Chase, wh—"

"Promise."

"All right." She still looked amused. She was so sure I was joking.

"Chase." There was an edge to Penny Cutler's voice. "I came here to do a story on you and your pie making. You are a talented young man. And you are interested—or so I thought—in building a career."

I thought of my mom mixing ingredients, tasting, retrying. Scribbling notes, smiling, the tip of her tongue sticking out the side of her mouth. A Leonardo da Vinci of the kitchen—just like I wanted to be with my pies.

"I *am* interested, ma'am. It means more to me than anything."

The TV reporter nodded. "Glad to hear it." She looked down at her notes.

"The first thing I would like to get on camera is you serving up a pie…"

Auntie was staggering past us on the way to her car. She glanced at me, at the TV reporter. She moved a little faster.

"…capture the swooning look on someone's face as they savor a Restless Pieman creation," Penny was saying.

"We need to stop Tilly McBride," I blurted.

Penny looked up in surprise.

I forced a cheery grin. "I mean, uh… Auntie owns Medusa's Scream. It would be cool to interview her. And she's leaving."

Penny tapped her fingers against her notepad. "That's a great idea, Chase. Hey! Maybe Tilly McBride could be the one who samples a Restless Pieman creation. We'd have the woman behind Auntie's Marmalade giving her blessing to the next generation. I can see this story going viral."

Penny ran off to catch Auntie.

Okay. I had delayed Auntie's escape. Now I had to somehow grab the jars from her. Twist off the lids and expose their sparkly contents for the TV camera.

Problem. I had no plan. I was like Bonnie Prince Charlie charging the English without his shield.

That made me turn and look at the train parked at the platform, soon to fill up with tourists. The shield on the front glistened in the morning sun. I liked the snakes. They looked fierce. They looked so don't-mess-with-us.

Auntie didn't like snakes. I remembered she had shuddered at the sight of them. *Enough to give you nightmares!*

Images jumbled in my mind. Not-so-sweet aunties with jars. Snakes. Shields. Charging the enemy.

Too bad I was a pieman, not a prince.

Or maybe *not* too bad.

I had an idea.

Chapter Fifteen

I jumped into the food truck. I tossed a new bottle of water to Lars. He and Sophie were gaping from me to the TV reporter, wondering what had happened to the interview.

I also grabbed the pie shell and crust that I had brought to make a comfort pie for Auntie and Sophie.

Before I'd discovered that it was Auntie, not Klopper, who was the mastermind behind the secret gold operation.

Auntie still deserved a pie. Penny Cutler was right. It would make great TV.

"I have to go get some pie ingredients," I told the camerawoman. "Please tell Penny I'll be right back."

The camerawoman grunted. She wiped sweat off her forehead and eyed Lars's water bottle.

Lars gripped the bottle tighter. He scowled back.

I grinned. I had been right about Lars. He was getting badder.

I ran to the gift shop.

Sophie called after me, "Chase, what's going on?"

"Remember your promise," I called back.

I wondered if she would. Things were about to get ugly.

Minutes later, freshly made pie in hand, I ran to the gate.

The TV reporter was holding her microphone up to Auntie. The camera-woman was filming.

Lars and Sophie watched from the side.

Sophie was smiling. I guessed she was thinking things were back on track. Poor kid. If she only knew her whole life was about to get derailed.

Lars clenched his water bottle. He was nervous, probably sensing a showdown.

At the sight of me Auntie's sweet smile grew strained. "Thank you for the interview, Ms. Cutler. I really must be go—"

Penny beamed. "Here's the Restless Pieman! He's made one of his creations just for you, Auntie! Isn't that right, Pieman?"

I cleared my throat. "I can honestly say I've never made this flavor before."

Penny let out a dramatic moan. "You are so lucky, Auntie. My son and I swoon for the Pieman's creations. Just wait until you sink your teeth into the buttery crust…the spices…the creamy texture…"

At this point I hesitated. I had told Penny the truth. A pie-making career did mean everything to me. It was my way of being creative. It was my way of staying close to my mom.

This TV spot could be my break. All I had to do was go back to the truck and get one of my regular pies. I would give Auntie a slice—and Penny too.

I didn't have to lose this big break. I could just tell the police what I had found out. Let them look into Auntie, Klopper and the hidden gold-filled stream and solve the mystery. I could be free and clear.

"Pieman?" Penny narrowed her eyes at me. As in, *Hurry up!*

I looked past Auntie to Sophie. Her eyes were bright. She was happy for me.

I started to tell them that I had to go back to the food truck for one last thing.

Then—a loud *pop!* Lars had clenched his bottle a little too hard. The plastic caved in. Water flew out, dousing Penny and the camerawoman.

Penny squealed. The camerawoman swore.

But it was Auntie I noticed. As the water flew, she let her sweet mask drop. She shot Lars a look of contempt.

I remembered what she had called Lars. *A loser. A nothing.*

"He's not nothing," I said aloud.

I stepped up to Auntie.

"Zoom in close!" Penny whispered to the camerawoman as she wiped off her microphone. "Remember—we're going for viral."

I held the pie up to Auntie's face. With my other hand I gripped the edge of the piecrust.

A roaring filled my ears. It was actually Klopper zooming his Mustang into the parking lot. But I didn't know that. To me it was Prince Charlie and his rebels yelling out their war cries as they charged the English.

Charlie had his shield. I had my pie.

I ripped the crust off the top of the pie. Black plastic snakes on springs sprang out at Auntie.

She screamed. She dropped the box.

The jars fell out, smashing against the cement path. Blood-orange marmalade rippled over the path like lava.

Gleaming from the oozing mess were chunky nuggets of gold.

Chapter Sixteen

Penny Cutler got her wish. The news story went viral. Last I checked, it had almost 100,000 hits on YouTube.

I'm just a blur at the start. Well, me and the flying snakes.

If you haven't seen the video, the camera zooms in on the nuggets. You hear Auntie's long, loud scream. It's piercing. It's Medusa-worthy.

The camera shows her running to her car and driving off in a whirl of dust.

She hasn't been seen since. Everyone figures she's hiding out somewhere, living off the money from the gold she stole.

Klopper didn't run. He confessed everything. It was like I suspected. He said he employed two kids no one else would hire. One who was scared and shy. One who acted out for attention. He thought grateful employees would be quiet employees.

Sophie's grandmother came to live with her. From what I hear, Granny is more fun than Auntie. She's teaching Sophie the Highland fling. I think a certain rebel prince would approve.

I've phoned Sophie a few times. She won't come to the phone. But I'll keep trying. She did promise she wouldn't stay mad forever.

Meanwhile, Medusa's Scream is closed while police and government lawyers investigate.

CBEE and other news outlets keep buzzing around the mine. People can't get enough of the story. Like Pete the Gold Panner says, everyone glitters with—well, you know.

I get the excitement over the gold find.

But it wasn't gold that saved me from falling down the mineshaft. It was friendship. It was Lars Fry.

Speaking of new friends, I never did take Sneeze Machine to the SPCA. Dad and I got used to having the Sneeze around.

Besides, with that haircut, who would ever adopt him?

As of this morning, it seems like I have another new friend.

I was biking through town when I heard someone yelling at me. "Hey, you! Troublemaker!"

Pete the Gold Panner shuffled up, thumbs tucked under his suspender straps.

I wondered what I had done. I hadn't laughed at his gold-panning tourists for a long time. With my right foot I spun the bike pedal, waiting for Pete to start scolding me.

He squinted. "So. Looks like I'm going to have some extra money coming in. Y'know, what with that stream you stumbled on."

He gestured at his store. "I was thinking of adding on a diner. I figure tourists get real hungry while they're panning for gold."

He took a moment to rub his bristly chin before continuing. "You be interested in serving up some of your pies?"

Acknowledgments

Warm thanks to my editor, Tanya Trafford, for her thoroughness and empathy in working with me on *Medusa's Scream*. And for making work seem not. Also to everyone at Orca for everything you do.

For those interested in reading more about the 1745 Scottish rebellion, I found Frank McLynn's biography *Bonnie Prince Charlie: Charles Edward Stuart* (Random House, 2003) especially informative. Unlike many historians, McLynn depicts Charlie not as a saint, not as a villain, but as an intriguing human being.

Melanie Jackson is the author of several Orca Currents titles, including *Death Drop* and *High Wire*. She likes hiking, piano, English/Scottish history—and continually learning from the kids she works with as a writing mentor with the Vancouver School Board. Melanie also teaches a mystery unit to grades eight and nine at two Vancouver secondary schools. She lives in Vancouver, British Columbia. For more information, visit melaniejacksonblog.wordpress.com.